For Zöe
(and Elzéard Bouffier)

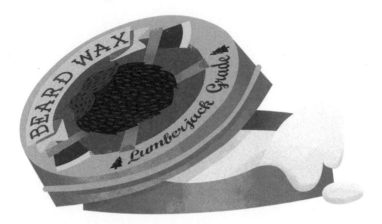

First U.S. edition 2017

Library of Congress Catalog Card Number pending
ISBN 978-0-7636-9649-8

17 18 19 20 21 22 TLF 10 9 8 7 6 5 4 3 2 1

Printed in Dongguan, Guangdong, China

This book was typeset in Clarendon BT and Factura.
The illustrations were created digitally.

TEMPLAR BOOKS

an imprint of
Candlewick Press
99 Dover Street
Somerville, Massachusetts 02144
www.candlewick.com

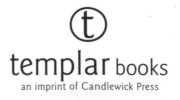

templar books
an imprint of Candlewick Press

THE LUMBERJACK'S BEARD

DUNCAN BEEDIE

Big Jim Hickory was a lumberjack.
He lived by the forest in a little log cabin.

He had burly shoulders
and a big, bristly beard.

Every morning,
he did limbering-up exercises.

(It's very important to limber up
if you're a lumberjack.)

After a hearty breakfast of pancakes and maple syrup,
Jim slung his trusty ax over his
burly shoulder and headed out into the forest.

CHOP-CHOPPETY-CHOP went Jim's ax,

echoing through the valley as he felled tree after tree after tree.

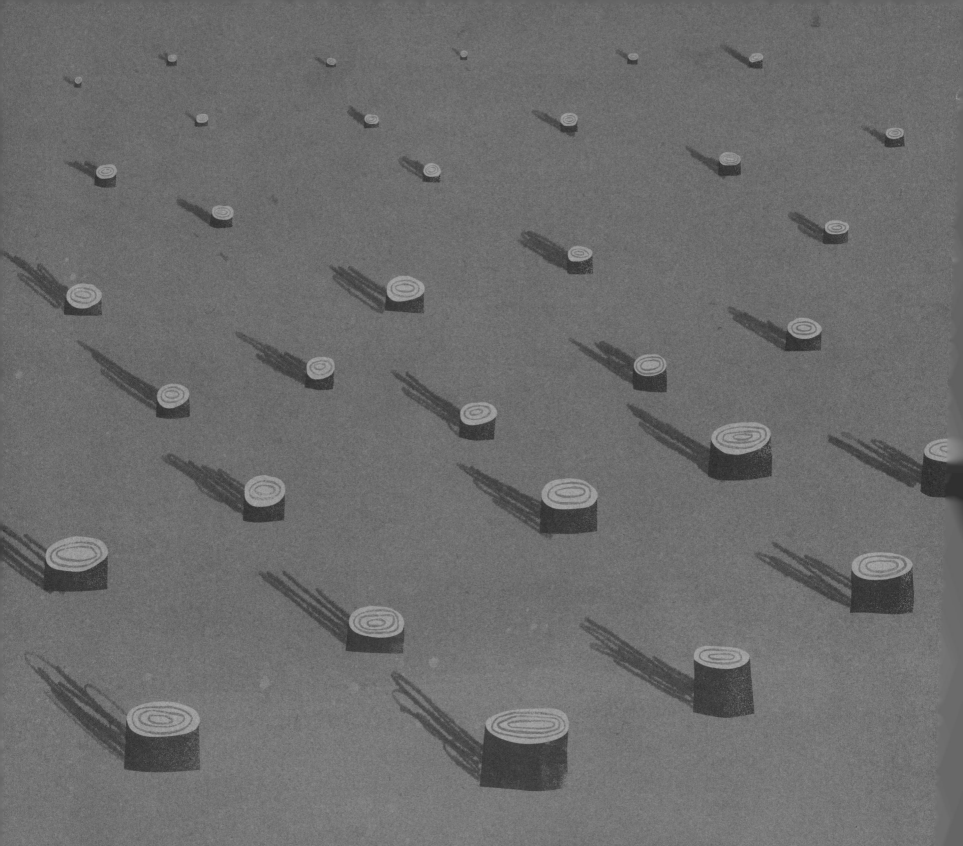

After a long day of swinging, whacking, cleaving, and hacking,

Jim headed back to his cabin.

That evening, when he was just about to go to bed,
he heard a **PECK-PECKITY-PECK** at the door.

Jim looked down to see a small and very angry bird. "I had just built
a new nest in my tree," shrieked the bird, "and you chopped it down!"

Jim scratched his chin. Then he had an idea.

"I suppose you could move into my beard," he said.

"Very well then!" said the bird, and in it flew.

The next morning, Jim woke up earlier than usual due to
the bird's chirping at the crack of dawn.

He did his limbering-up exercises, got dressed, and ate his breakfast
(with a little help from the new tenant in his beard).

Jim's next job was to strip all the branches and leaves
from the tree trunks and burn them in a big bonfire.

After a long day of chopping, snapping, burning, and crackling,
Jim trudged back to his cabin for a well-earned rest.

No sooner had he put away his ax
than he heard a noise at the door:
SCRATCH-SCRATCHETY-SCRATCH.
He looked down to see a very
angry porcupine.

"I needed those leaves and pine
needles to make a cozy shelter, but you
burned them. Where am I going to live
now?" snapped the porcupine.

Jim thought and scratched his chin.

"Well," he said, "I suppose you could move into my beard."

He bent down and the porcupine crawled in.

The next morning, Jim woke even earlier and
attempted to do his limbering-up exercises. He looked
in the mirror and scratched his chin.

YOOOOOWWWW! He got porcupine quills in his fingers.

He tried to eat his breakfast . . .

but lost his appetite when he noticed bird poop on his shirt.

Jim's job that day was to float all the
tree trunks down the river to the lumberyard.
One by one, he rolled the logs into
the fast-flowing water.

After a hard day of lugging, splashing,
rolling, and crashing . . .

Jim staggered back to his cabin.

THWUMP-THWUMPETY-THWUMP went his door.

He looked down to see a very angry beaver on his doorstep.

"I spent all day building my dam, and it got

smashed to bits by those logs you threw in the river!" it snarled.

Without a word, Jim picked up the beaver and put it in his beard.

Between the bird's chirping, the porcupine's prickling, and the beaver's thwumping, Jim didn't get much sleep that night.

He was too tired to do his limbering-up exercises in the morning, and the beaver's thwumping tail knocked his pancakes all over the floor.

"That's it!" cried Jim. "I can't take it anymore!
You all have to move out today!"

"BUT WHERE WILL WE LIVE?"
cried the animals.

As Jim scratched his chin, he had a brilliant idea.
He went into his bathroom, took out a razor,
and began to shave off his big, bristly beard.

Then he took the hair and piled it up on his porch, and the bird, the porcupine, and the beaver all moved into their big, bristly new den.

That night, Jim slept better than
he had for some time.

He woke up and did some particularly
vigorous limbering-up exercises and
put on a fresh plaid shirt.

Then he made an enormous tower
of pancakes and maple syrup.

Jim looked out the window at the bare ground where the forest used to be and scratched his now-stubbly chin.

Then he had another brilliant idea.

Jim took his shovel
and dug hole after hole after hole . . .

and planted tree after tree after tree.

Jim's beard grew back over time.

The trees took quite a bit longer . . .

but it was worth the wait.

THE END

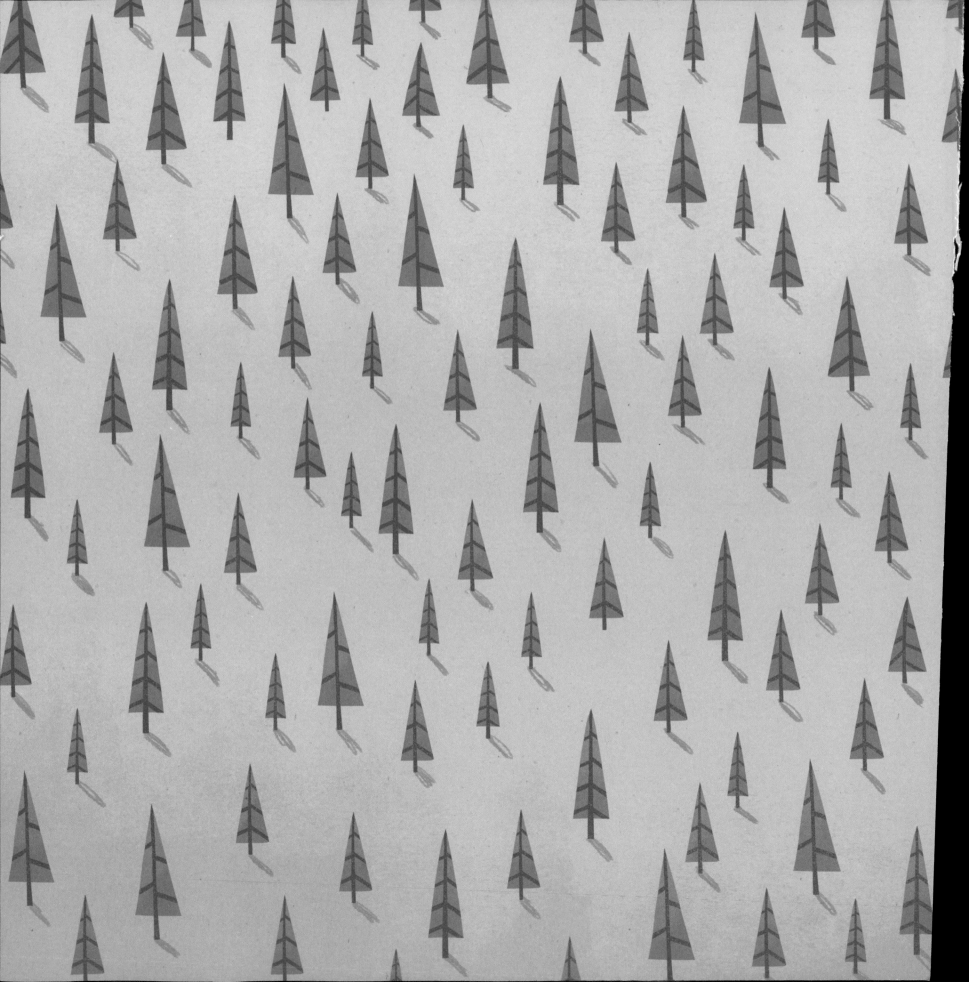